Tease

A Collection of Short Erotic Fiction

By LJB Novels

Tease

By

LJB Novels

This book is a work of fiction. Names, characters, places, and incidents, other than those clearly in terms public domain, are the product of the author's imagination or used fictitiously. Any resemblance to actual persons, living or dead, business establishments, events, or locations is entirely coincidental.

Contents

Take Your Punishment

This was how it all began, our relationship. There had been countless messages on various apps. Flirtatious messages, sexy messages, serious messages. Messages that discussed the boundaries and allowed us to get to know one another better. But now I sat in his car, excited and nervous as I stared down at my hands. He had taken me out for dinner and made sure that we both wanted the same thing. I had followed his requests by wearing a cute dress with black stockings and no underwear. There was no question in my mind. I wanted this.

Arriving at his home he brought me inside and made sure that I was comfortable, and I relaxed. It wasn't long before, his lips pressed against mine, his tongue slipping across my lips but as they parted, he pulled away from me, smirking.

'On your hands and knees, on the floor.' He whispered. I quickly slipped off the sofa onto the floor, getting into position. I could feel his presence as he knelt behind me, bunching up my dress at my waist. I jumped when I felt his cold hands on my backside.

'You've managed to rack up quite a tally,' he mocked, 'What was it?' He gave my ass a squeeze to make sure I was listening.

'17,' I said, I could feel his breath on my ear as he leaned over me.

'It's Sir, from now on, understand?' He asked, I nodded.

'Yes, Sir.' Out of the corner of my eye, I could see him smirk as he straightened up again.

'You will count every single one of them.'

'Yes, Sir.'

The first slap came unexpectedly, making me jump forward slightly and the carpet grazed my skin. Sir paused, waiting

'One Sir,' I said.

'Good girl.' He smiled, continuing the slaps, alternating between each cheek until I counted 10. He paused to caress my ass, soothing the warm, red skin. I slowly rubbed my thighs together, feeling the arousal dripping down my legs.

'I have something else. Don't move.' He ordered, leaving my side and walking towards the cupboard, I listened to him rustling until the cupboard closed.

I had no idea what he had, but Sir returned to my side, jumped feeling cold wood against my ass.

'Keep counting.' He ordered, running the wooden instrument across my ass cheeks, soothing the skin. He pulled the paddle away from me and brought it back down across both my ass cheeks. The sharp pain made me cry out, leaving a stinging sensation. I shuddered, the pain only intensifying my arousal.

'Count.' Sir commanded.

'Eleven Sir.' I choked out, my ass stinging but my pussy was dripping wet. He repeated the action twice more, making me jolt forward into the carpet.

'Twelve and thirteen, Sir.' He paused to massage my ass soothing and enhancing the sting in the same motion. One more paddle on each ass cheek brought the total up to fifteen. Two more to go.

I expected Sir to continue with the paddle, but I heard it dropped on the floor, and he picked up something else. My whole body shuddered when I felt the cool leather of a riding crop tapping against my clit.

'Count them, girl.' He ordered, the riding crop coming down across my ass and making me cry out.

'Count them!' He warned.

'Seventeen Sir.' I spat out, realising the mistake too late.

'Oh dear,' Sir said, 'what happened to sixteen?'

'I'm sorry Sir.' I whispered,

'Let's try that again.' The riding crop struck my ass harder.

'Sixteen Sir!' I cried out.

'Good girl,' He said, bringing the crop down once more.

'Seventeen Sir!' I whispered. My body was on fire from my stinging ass.

My dripping pussy clenched around nothing, desperate to be touched. I flinched and cried out when I felt something cold against my ass, it soothed the sting but made me shudder. Sir rubbed what I assumed was ice across my ass and down my pussy. I almost screamed when he shoved the ice inside pushing it as far as it could go with his fingers. My body shook as he moved his fingers inside me, I was already so wet, and it didn't take long to reach my peak.

Sir pulled his fingers out of me and I whined in protest. But it quickly turned to a moan as his fingers were replaced by his cock. Grabbing my hips he thrust into me, my end quickly approaching. Sir weaved his fingers into my hair and tugged my head backwards, making my back arch.

'Please can I cum Sir?' I cried out, unsure whether I would be able to hold out any longer.

'Yes.' He growled, he didn't even have to finish the word before I came with a cry. He continued to thrust into me, dragging out my orgasm until I collapsed forward, unable to hold myself up anymore.

Sir leaned across my back, moving my hair from my face and biting my earlobe. 'It's not over yet, we still have a whole night ahead of us.'

I felt the ice melt completely, leaving a wet tingling sensation in my pussy. He gently took my hands, pulling to back up into the sitting position. He wrapped a blanket around my shoulders and smiled warmly. He handed me a glass of water and helped me up, smirking when he saw the bruises already blossoming on my ass.

'On the bed.' He ordered, taking the empty glass away. I crawled onto the bed and laid on my back, my head between the pillows, groaning as I felt the smooth sheets on my sensitive skin. Sir took each of my wrists and used a rope to tie them to both bedposts, tickling my palms to ensure it wasn't too tight. He did the same with my ankles so I was spread eagle on the bed. Sir smiled at his handy work and pulled fabric out of his bag. I quickly realised that it was an eye mask, he slipped it over my head. Everything went black.

I felt the bed dip as Sir sat between my legs. There was a moment of silence and my mind raced. But everything went blank when I felt his hands on my breasts, pinching and pulling at my nipples. I squealed and writhed so much the sleeping mask came off my eyes. Sir sighed and got off the bed.

'Little squirmer.' He mumbled, my eyes followed him as he reached into his bag, pulling out a scarf. 'Need to make sure it stays on...' Sir wrapped the scarf around my head, covering my eyes, nose and mouth, tying a knot behind my head.

Sir settled between my legs again, toying with my nipples. He leaned over my body, gently kissing my neck and shoulder until I relaxed in my restraints. He kissed down my chest, making me hum in pleasure. I shrieked when he bit the underside of my breast, but it didn't stop him from biting and massaging both breasts before moving down until his fingers found my pussy lips. I pulled and tugged at the bindings, but his mouth continued to move down, biting and sucking my ribs, hip and stomach. With the scarf still tied around my head, all I could do was squirm and cry out, my own arousal growing with each bit and each movement of his fingers.

I whined when his hands and mouth left my skin. My orgasm was so close, it would only take a light touch to make me come. Sir lay down on the bed next to me and removed the scarf. His fingers ran back down to my pussy, only lightly tapping it, but with my sensitivity, my hips jolted upwards, the slightest touch sending me closer to the edge. My body lifted, and I moaned when he lightly slapped my clit. Sir repeated the action, harder, I moaned again. He continued slapping my clit, the sensation driving me right to the edge and almost tipping me over. But I fell back, knowing the trouble I'd get into if I didn't ask.

'Please can I cum Sir?' My voice barely above a whisper, my pussy clenching as I tried to hold back.

'You're a little masochist, aren't you?' He chuckled.

'Please Sir, I need to come...' I cried.

'Not yet.' He ordered. I screamed as I tried to hold myself, continuing to beg.

'Please Sir! Please let me cum!'

'You may.' He didn't even need to finish before I let everything go, screaming as my orgasm washed over me. He quickly shoved two fingers into me, I clenched around them and he rubbed his thumb across my clit, dragging it out.

I relaxed against the bed, panting as he pulled his finger out, smiling down at me.

'I never knew how much of a masochist you were.' I didn say anything, just lay trying to catch my breath, lazily smiling u at   hin

'Good girl.' He smiled, pressing a kiss to my lip

Permission

Sir had kept me waiting for so long without release. It ha only been a week, but every single day he had made me edge Pushing myself right to the brink before stopping, leaving m pleading, needing. Most of the time I did it to myself, he wouldn touch me. So many times, I thought of disobeying him, but couldn't. I wouldn't. The punishment would only be worse. Th thought of it made me wet so easily. I shivered. Sir began makin demands: sneaking photos in public places, wearing toys whenever I went out, but the marker was his favourite.

He would order me to write on my body, either his name or some other words he used to describe me. I wrote them in places that could be seen upon his instruction.

Through all of that, it was the phone calls that nearly tipped me over the edge. Every night Sir would call We would have our usual conversations, and then I had to listen to him tell me every little detail of what he would do to me. I would beg for permission to relieve the ache I felt after every conversation. He never granted it.

Now Sir was here, taking me into his arms drawing me into a long kiss as his hands wandered my body. His body lay next to mine on the bed, Sir's hands moved down to my shorts, beginning to rub my pussy through them.

'Get them off.' He ordered as he pulled away, I quickly unbuttoned my shorts and pushed them down, kicking them off my ankles. Sir closed the distance again and continued to kiss down my neck, mumbling into my skin.

'I missed you.' His fingers found my clit, his free hand coming up to pinch my nipple through my bra. I moaned and arched to him. Pulling away, Sir reached into the box by the side of the bed. He pulled out the vibrator and pressed it to my clit on the highest setting.

I squirmed beneath the vibrator. All the edging meant my body responded quickly and the pleasure built up fast. My head fell back as my eyes fluttered shut, giving myself to the pleasure for just a moment.

'Please, can I cum Sir?' I begged, feeling my legs beginning to shake as I balled my fists into his shirt.

'If you can look me in the eye as you do.'

I pulled my head forward and opened my eyes, looking Sir in the eye as the pleasure coursed through me. I tried to keep my eyes open, but Sir pulled the vibrator away from my clit and pushed two fingers into me, beginning to thrust and drag out my orgasm. My back arched, and I cried out, squeezing my eyes shut.

When he pulled his fingers out I fell limp on the bed, Sir dragged his wet fingers up my body, pushing them into my mouth. I wasted no time licking them clean, the lower half of my body still twitching.

Sir got off the bed and motioned me to follow.

'Come on.' He pulled me up and turned me to face away from him. 'Strip.'

I pulled off my top and quickly undid my bra, discarding them I was completely nude in front of him. Goose bumps prickled along my skin, apart from the cold air, part because I could still feel Sir's presence behind me, making me wait. With one hand on my hip, his other gently pushed between my shoulder blades, bending me over the edge of the bed. His foot tapped against my ankles, nudging them apart.

'Arms behind your back.' Sir ordered. I quickly folded my arms behind my back, grabbing the opposite elbow and waited. I jumped when I felt the soft leather or the riding crop against my ass.

'It has been too long.' Sir whispered, dragging the crop along my skin. I squealed when the first strike came down on my right cheek. It was quickly followed by Sir rubbing his clothed cock against my ass. The second strike made my yelp,   my reflexes closed my legs, my hands fell to cover my bum, but I quickly moved back to my original position. Sir didn't trust my instincts. Kneeling behind me, he secured leather cuffs around my ankles, attaching them to a rope. When he was finished, I slowly moved my feet, hearing the clink of the metal bar that he secured to my ankles, keeping my legs apart. Satisfied, Sir continued with the crop three more times, I could feel the bruises forming on my ass.

Sir leaned over me, rubbing his clothed cock against my pussy, the abrasive denim was a delicious mix of arousal and irritation. Pulling away, he unbuttoned his trousers and grabbed my wrists. He yanked my hips against him as he pushed into me with a moan. Sir's forearm pressed against my back as he leaned over me, keeping me pinned. Every thrust pushed me into the side of the bed. The only thing that mattered was how quickly my orgasm was approaching.

My legs began to shake as I tried to keep them open, the temptation to fight against the bar and just let go was becoming too much. The idea of disobeying was almost too enticing. Taking in sharp breaths as the pleasure continued to build more and more. Just as I was reaching the brink of my orgasm, Sir pulled out and delivered a swift slap to my ass.

'On the bed.' He commanded.

I quickly crawled onto the bed, lying with my head between the pillows. Sir followed with the vibrator in hand, sitting between my legs. My orgasm was slowly slipping away as Sir flicked the vibrator on and pressed it against my clit.

The pleasure came rushing back.

'Please, can I cum Sir?'

'Not yet. 60... 59... 58...' Sir counted down, the wand buzzing harshly against my clit.

Count faster you bastard! My mind screamed, my breathing becoming uneven as I tried to hold back the orgasm threatening to break. I was so close to failing miserably.

'Cum without permission and it's 25 with the crop.' Sir reminded me, I shivered at the thought of it. The previous welts still burned, and I was unsure how I felt about getting more. Shivers of arousal were sent straight down to my core at the thought of the riding crop again, the mixture of pain and pleasure were too alluring.

I balled my fists into the sheets as I focused on Sir words again, listening to his countdown, only just reaching 20.

'Fuck. Fuck. Fuck. Fuck.' The words fell from my lips. stared up at the ceiling trying to hold back. I started counting the cracks in the paint.

O-One… Another one… Another one… A crack there. FUCK. Even the voice in my head stuttered, I gave up after reaching four and focused on Sir's words. Listening for h permission.

'3… 2… 1… Cum now.'

I screamed as soon as he reached one, my whole-body convulsing with pleasure. Sir's hand spread across my stomach holding the vibrator against my clit.

As my body relaxed, Sir pulled the vibrator away from m clit and I fell limp onto the bed. Sir smiled, watching my chest ris and fall with each stuttered breath. My head rolled to the side eyes fluttering shut as Sir allowed me a moment to collect myself

'Good girl.' He discarded the vibrator and grabbed m hips, rolling me over onto my stomach. I pulled my knees under me so my ass was in the air. He pulled my hips back, pushing into my pussy. Sir pressed his hands against my shoulder blades for support as he began to thrust, pushing me further into the bed. My already sensitive walls clenched and twitched around him, each thrust drew a moan from my lips, my third orgasm of the night building.

A whine escaped me when he pulled out, tapping my ass.

'I want you on top.' He reclined on the bed. I shuffled over and swung my leg over his hip. I could feel the orgasm slipping away. Slowly, I sunk down onto him, bracing my hands on his chest and beginning to bounce. My focus was on regaining that blissful orgasm.

Sir was unhappy with my efforts. He grabbed my hips to stop me and started thrusting up into me. Falling forward, I braced my hands on the headboard, giving Sir the opportunity to take one of my nipples into his mouth, biting harshly. I cried out and held into the headboard, feeling the pleasure building.

'Please, Sir! Please can I cum?' I begged, unsure how long I would be able to hold it. Sir released my hips, choosing to pinch both of my nipples. The sensation made me cum before I even had permission. Sir continued to thrust, moaning as he came inside me.

I collapsed on top of Sir, rolling off him onto the bed. He gently pushed on my shoulder, and rolled me until I was facing away from him and drew me close until my back was pressed against his chest. His arm slipped beneath my head as a makeshift pillow and I cuddled into him. My body relaxed at his touch. I could feel his hand on my hip, his fingers rubbing small circles as he whispered in my ear.

'What did I say about cumming without permission?'

Shit.

Rule Breaker

Sir had let me off for the night. He didn't say anything about it the next day either. I knew something was going to happen, but he loved to make me wait. Everything was as usual that morning. We had breakfast together and he went off the work, leaving me with a day of tasks both of domestic and sexual to complete.

Cleaning the kitchen while wearing a butt plug - with photo evidence, edging myself before cleaning the bathroom, wearing nothing but nipple clamps and an apron while cleaning the living room. By the time he came home, everything was clean, and I was dressed in a skirt and vest top.

Sir sat down on the sofa, calling me over to him.

'Turn and show me your bruises.' He ordered, I quickly turned to face away from him and pulled up my skirt, revealing the dark purple bruises on my ass.

'Still tender?' He asked the question was made redundant when he pressed his thumb onto one of my bruises, dragging a yelp from my lips and making me jump forward. Glancing over my shoulder I could see that Sir was smiling, even the smallest yelp turned him on; the thought of more bruises began to send small waves of arousal through my body.

His fingers grabbed my hips, pulling me down to sit on his lap. Sir's thighs pressed onto my bruises, instantly making me squirm. His hands moved down to open my legs, his fingers moving up my skin to my pussy, rubbing up and down my lips until he started to focus on my clit. I leaned back into him, resting my hand on his wrist as Sir's other hand pulled my top and bra down, pinching my nipple and making my back arch.

With Sir's fingers on my clit, his hand on my breast and breath on my neck, I could feel my orgasm approaching fast. The moans that slipped from my lips must have told Sir the same.

'You came without permission last night, do that again and you'll regret it.' He warned. I nodded, barely paying attention to his words, too focused on his fingers to care.

'Can I please cum, Sir?' I whispered, feeling myse
on the edge.

'No.' Sir said, removing his hand from my clit.
whine escaped my lips, but it quickly turned into a scream as h
hands came down to smack my pussy. I bent forward, my hand
come down to cover myself as the mix of pain and pleasur
radiated through me.

Sir pushed me off his lap and pulled me to his side
his thumb rubbing across my arm.

'It's not over yet.' He whispered, pulling me off th
sofa with him. My pussy still stung as I walked, the edge c
orgasm gone but the arousal was still there.

Together we went upstairs to the bedroom. Sir stoppe
me in front of the bed and held me against him, his hands goin
back to my breast and pussy. He brought me back to the brink c
orgasm before pulling away. Sir's hand on my back bent me ove
the bed and I quickly spread my legs, feeling his hands runnin
over my ass. I heard him chuckle as poked one of the bruise
again, watching me squirm. He gave a quick slap to the leas
bruised cheek and made me yelp.

'I have to make sure they match.' He reasoned. I waited patiently waited as Sir stripped, out of the corner of my eye I could see him pick up the riding crop.

Pushing the skirt up to my waist, he ran the leather across my ass. A few light taps were followed by a hard hit on my ass, making me jerk forward. His fingers quickly found my clit and the sting was almost completely forgotten about, he wanted to keep me permanently on edge.

'Get on the bed.' Sir ordered. I quickly complied, lying flat on my stomach. He followed with something in his hands and dropped it onto me. It was cold. Metal. Grabbing my wrists, he pulled them behind my back, and I realised what they were. Handcuffs.

With my hands securely behind my back, Sir climbed onto the bed, gathering my hair into a ponytail and lifted my head. Sir knelt in front of me, his hard cock level with my face. I wasted no time opening my mouth as much of him in as I could. He began to snap his hips into me, gripping my hair tightly. Sir groaned with every thrust and I began to squirm, becoming desperate for more attention on my pussy. I could tell he was watching me, so I began to wiggle my ass, hoping to send the right signals.

Sir pulled out of me and climbed off the bed, opening the drawer hidden in the side of it. I saw three things get pulled out from the corner of my eye before the drawer was closed Sir picked up the vibrator and flicked it on, putting it against my clit and closed my legs to keep it there. He climbed back on the bed and sat on my legs, rendering me immobile.

I felt a tickle on my ass that I instantly recognised; it was the lighter side of the wooden paddle. I waited for the harsh side to come, but it still shocked me when it did. I cried out and tried to roll onto my side, but I was stuck. Sir pushed my hip back down to lay flat and continued with the paddle across both cheeks, avoiding the older bruises and creating brand new ones on my hips and thighs. The vibrator pressed harshly against my clit, the pleasure building but the pain keeping me from the edge. I squirmed and screamed.

Soon it was all too much. The pleasure was too much, and I had waited so long.

'Please Sir can I cum?' I begged. Sir acknowledged my pleas by turning the vibrator setting down, the lower pulse keeping me on edge, but was all it did. The feathers sent a ticklish sensation across my ass, but it still stung when he swatted it against my skin. Out of instinct, my hands moved down to cover my ass, soon there would be no room left for new bruises.

'Don't cover yourself,' he warned, 'I'll make it worse.' He swatted the paddle down onto my right thigh, proving his point as I jumped and screamed.

Bucking my hips downwards onto the vibrator, I could feel my orgasm approaching once more.

'Please, can I cum Sir?' I asked again.

'Five more and you can.' He brought the paddle down once on each cheek as he spoke, pausing and making me wait for the next three. I continued to squirm as each hit came down, my instincts taking over. Two hits came down on the same cheek and I screamed out, waiting for the final one.

'Keep still for the last one otherwise you won't cum.' He warned. I swallowed and nodded, waiting for the final hit. It came across the middle of my ass, making me scream, tears falling down my cheeks. I took in shallow breaths as Sir discarded the paddle and leaned over my body, his hand moving under my leg and flicking the vibrator back onto its highest setting.

'Cum for me.' He commanded. I cried out as I came. The pleasure, all the sensitivity, all the pain, I felt it all in one moment.

Sir climbed off me, moving to kneel in front of my face once more, his fingers weaving into my hair as he pulled me up and onto his cock. My mind was completely blank as I let him use me, thrusting into my mouth until he came, releasing a growl as I swallowed everything.

He uncuffed me and rolled me onto my back, grabbing my attention.

'What have we learned today?' He asked, I smiled up at him.

'Don't cum without permission.' I whispered.

'Good girl.'

On Your Knees

It was just the two of us alone all day. He was working from home, and I wanted to test the waters, push him to see how far I could get. Sir would ignore me because of his work, but our agreement said I had to be around and ready whenever he wanted me. Usually, I would spend the day watching TV or doing my own work, but today I was rummaging through my bag until I found what I was looking for. Bright red lacy lingerie with a matching harness. Once it was on, I stood in front of the mirror admiring my reflection. I grabbed one of Sir's shirts and slipped it over, only closing the two middle buttons; the shirt was see-through over the red harness. I smirked to myself.

Walking back into the living room I felt Sir's eyes on me, following me across the room as I headed towards the kitchen, ignoring his computer. I had my back to him as I prepared my breakfast, but I could feel his eyes on me, burning into my back as I 'accidentally' dropped a grape, I crossed my ankles and be

at the waist to show him my thong. I could hear Sir's chair sque

as he turned back to his computer, trying his best to ignore me

opened the cupboard and reached up to the top shelf – S

always kept the bowls there for this reason – as I reached up

grab a bowl the shirt rode up to reveal the bottom of the harnes

around my hips. Turning back, I caught him staring. Sir turne

back to his computer quickly, and I smirked at my littl

achievement. I brewed the coffee and grabbed a mug and bov

of fruit, heading towards him.

'You shouldn't work on an empty stomach.' I smile

sweetly, leaning over him to place the bowl and coffee mug o

the desk by Sir's keyboard, making sure to press my breast

against his back.

'Thank you.' He smiled, his hands not moving from th

keyboard.

'You're very welcome.' I pressed a lingering kiss to hi

cheek, my hands sliding down his shoulders and across hi

chest. I felt him inhale, trying to control himself before I pulle

away, heading back to the kitchen to start my own breakfast.

As I made myself tea, I could tell Sir's eyes were on me as he did his work, he couldn't help but glance over. I kept my cool, ignoring him as I made myself comfortable on the sofa, bringing my knees to my chest and unbuttoning the top half of the shirt, letting it fall open to reveal the harness.

This continued all morning. I made sure that everything I did would keep his attention. Sir took a lunch break halfway through the day, I met him in the kitchen, leaning over the counter and crossed my arms, pushing my chest up. Sir shuffled uncomfortably as he got more coffee but said nothing on returning to his desk. I scowled. I wanted to kick and scream on the floor like a child, but I just continued my plan. Walking into the living room with coffee in my hand, I stood next to him as he worked.

'You shouldn't work too hard; you'll end up with a headache.' I smiled, he leaned back in his chair and rubbed his forehead.

'Already there.' Sir mumbled.

'Oh dear!' I put down the coffee mug and pushed his chair further out, sliding to sit on his lap, I couldn't help but smile just a little when I felt his half-hard cock through his trousers.

'I need to get these done for the meeting later,' he said, grabbing my hips and trying to push me off his lap.

'A little break won't hurt.' I smiled, gently rubbing his shoulders and neck.

'Mmmm.' He replied, his cock twitching in his trousers. 'I have work to do.' Sir pushed harder on my hips and pushed me off his lap, tucking his chair in and working.

I scoffed and grabbed my mug, storming away. I wasn't giving up that easily. I carried on all afternoon; moving so that Sir could see down the shirt, bending over to show my panties, even a stretch and yawn to make sure he would notice me. I wanted him to break, I wanted to see how far I could push him. As the afternoon came to an end and Sir's meeting neared, I found I was bored. He had managed to stay at his computer all day. No comment. No touching. Nothing.

Eventually, I gave up, walking back to the bedroom to change, as I walked passed him, I exaggerated the sway of my hips, one last hope in making him break. But nothing, I pulled off his shirt and threw it onto the bed. I reached behind my back to unhook my bra when I felt two hands grab my wrists and pull me backwards. I crashed into Sir's chest, feeling his hard cock against my ass.

'You think you can do this all day and not face consequences?' Sir growled, his lips coming down on my skin to bite and suck on my neck, a moan slipped from my lips. He pulled away from me and pushed me against the wall. My hand instantly went toward my panties, but Sir grabbed it.

'Don't even think about it.' He growled, yanking my hand away from my panties. He pulled the cups of my bra down and grabbed my breasts, roughly kneading them as moans slipped passed my lips.

'Get on your knees.' Sir ordered.

I obediently sunk to the floor, my back against the wall. Sir practically ripped his trousers open and pushed them halfway down his thighs with his boxers, grabbing his half-hard cock and beginning to stroke it.

'Hands.' Sir snapped, I lifted my hands above my head, feeling arousal burning in my core as he grabbed my wrists with one hand, holding them against the wall.

'Open your legs.' I moved to balance on my toes, opening my legs and resting my ass on my heels. He smiled at his view.

Now fully hard, Sir grabbed his cock and ran the tip along my lips.

'Open.' He ordered. I parted my lips without hesitation, letting my jaw go slack so he could do as he pleased. Sir pressed me against the wall as his cock passed my lips, and the tip hit the back of my throat. I forced back my gag reflex and didn't move as he snapped his hips forward, the tip of his cock repeatedly hitting the back of my throat. Sir moaned as I moved my tongue around his cock, his free hand moving to caress my cheek.

I wiggled my fingers in his grip as it got tighter, holding me up as he thrusts became harsh and unforgiving, almost knocking me off balance multiple times. Sir moaned above me, his hand leaving my face to press against the wall, keeping his own balance as he thrust into me. Tears began to roll down my cheeks; my lungs burned and I tried to pull my head away, but the wall stopped me from moving. Realising there was a problem, Sir pulled out of my mouth; I gasped for air, taking in large gulps. His hand pumped his dick as I caught my breath, and I swallowed the spit that hadn't dribbled from my mouth. Sir's hand left his cock and grabbed my chin, pulling my mouth open again. I let my jaw go slack again as I took one last gulp of air. He pushed his cock back into my mouth, his rhythm getting faster again. Sir's tip hitting the back of my throat once again, his free hand pinching my nose and stopping me breathing as he rammed his cock down my throat. Tears began to fall down my cheeks again, struggling to breathe.

Sir's grip tightened on my wrists and his thrusts grew faster and clumsy. There was no warning as he came, pulling out of my mouth and shooting his cum across my face; I felt my legs shaking from the strain as I tried to hold myself up in the same position. Sir moaned as the final spurts of cum dripped onto my chin. He rubbed his cock along my face, collecting his cum and pushing it into my mouth. Sir smirked as I obediently swallowed what he gave me.

Sir pulled his trousers back up and knelt in front of m

smirking at my face. He grabbed chin between his thumb ar

forefinger.

'Face the consequences.' He smirked, pulling his han

away and slapped my pussy; I cried out and my legs gave wa

falling into a heap on the floor. The arousal was only mad

worse; a wet spot was now visible on my red panties. He smirke

and stood.

'Gotta get to that meeting.' He smiled. 'Don't you move

He had me on the floor, taking in gulps of air as my makeup ra

down my cheeks. The uncomfortable wetness in my panties onl

getting worse as I had to wait for him to return.

Bruises

She pushed the sheets from her body, the soft materi

brushing against her skin. The sun was just peeking through th

curtains. The bed was empty next to her but the sound of runnin

water promised he was still there. She stretched her arms abov her head, feeling the familiar soreness from the night before. Swinging her legs out of the bed, she smiled down at them. Standing up, she moved to the mirror.

He was an artist in the bedroom and her body was covered with his craft. She stared at her reflection in the mirror, her eyes scanning over every bruise that littered her skin. Last night he had shamelessly made her beg, made her moan, made her his. Her wrists and ankles still had the indentation from the leather straps; the soft padding only protected the skin from so much. The only time the straps were removed was when he wanted her to turn over. The implements were still on the floor, carefully piled together in the corner.

The riding crop had left the bruises on her legs; the leather had sparked a sharp sting on her skin with every hit, but now they were almost square-shaped bruises littered across thighs. They stopped at the knee, where additional restraints had been needed to stop her from pulling away from the crop. Before he set that down for the night, he had put it to her feet; she'd complained that they were too cold and needed to be warmed up.

It hadn't been what she'd had in mind, but it worked. She still felt the soles of her feet tingle with every step.

Turning in the mirror, she admired her red stripes from the cane it wasn't quite hard enough to leave a bruise, but those red marks would be there for a couple of days at least, a gentle reminder whenever she sat down. The thin wooden cane was leaning up against the mirror; the impact of each strike burned, but it wasn't until after the cane left her skin that she felt its bite. The sting of the cane made her legs shake with every strike. That was last night; now the cane strikes were perfectly straight, but were almost covered by the two large purple bruises of the paddle.

The wooden paddle was a horrible implement. Each strike leaving its own bruise on top of her already sore ass. It was nearing the end of the night, orgasms throughout making her sensitive. At the end he had brought that out, dragging the screams from her lips with every strike. He had added a strap around her waist to keep her still, creating an easy target for him.

While the bruises where prominent along her skin, she thought about the night before. How she asked to be hit again.

How not once did she even think about uttering the safe word, to stop all the pain. Instead, she relished in it, begging for more through the tears. Pleading for it to not stop until she was well and truly spent. And as always, he would never refuse.

Headaches

He sat at his computer staring at the screen despite the building pressure across his forehead, a dull, aching pain growing prominent. He looked over his shoulder at the beauty that sat on the settee, her legs tucked beneath her body, wearing one of his shirts as she read through his most recent manuscript, a red pen in hand. She felt his gaze on her and looked up, smiling when their eyes met. He only returned a small smile and turned back to his computer, turning the brightness of the screen down trying to soothe his head.

Frowning at his actions, she abandoned the manuscript and pen on the coffee table, getting up and walking to stand behind him; her thin fingers slipped under the collar of his shirt, dancing gently along his skin, her touch getting firmer on beginning to rub his shoulders.

'Are you okay?' She asked, he sighed and stopped typing, his head falling into his hands, rubbing his sore eyes.

'I feel another headache coming on.'

She pulled her hands out from his shirt and grabbed the back of the chair, rolling it out from under the desk, giving her just enough room to slip in front of him and slide into his lap, straddling his waist with a leg on either side of his thighs; she wrapped her arms around him, gently running her fingers through his hair.

'Mmmm, this is nice.' His hands moved from the arms of the chair to her body, immediately moving under her shirt and ghosting across her hips, to her ass. His arms tightened around her, pulling her close and pressing his face between her breasts.

'Still feeling the headache?' She asked, gently running her fingers through his hair. He nodded and mumbled something that was muffled by her shirt, he pulled away for just a moment to feather kisses along the top of her cleavage.

'Hey.' She whispered.

'Yes?' He asked, continuing to kiss along her collar bone, straining his neck to reach hers and find the sweet spot that drove her crazy, biting down hard and sucking a mark into her skin.

She let out a small moan and weaved her fingers into his hair, beginning to tug gently. Taking her actions as encouragement, he began to unbutton the shirt she wore revealing the matching set of blue lace bra and panties beneath. Smiling, he ran his hands up her sides, pushing the sides of the shirt out of the way and kissing up her neck until she finally leaning down and pressed their lips together, pouring all her passion into a single kiss. His hands moved to undo her bra, her hands were tugging at the hem of his shirt, only breaking the kiss for a second to pull his shirt over his head and throw it over his shoulder.

She could feel his cock beginning to twitch against his trousers, smirking at how quickly he became aroused. She bucked her hips down, rubbing her panty covered pussy against his cock, restricted by his denim jeans. Her hands ran up his chest feeling every muscle tense with even a slight movement as he did the same, finding every curve and dip. She could feel his hard cock against her, between her legs as she ground down onto him, feeling wetness grow in her own panties.

She moaned as she ground down against him, letting him push the shirt off her shoulders, the linen piling at their feet as he focused on the bra, pulling it off of her and throwing it over his shoulders. Her breasts bounced free, only for his hands to cup, them and he began pinching her nipples. Her back arched to him and he took the opportunity to take one of her nipples into his mouth. His free hand moved down and slipped beneath her panties.

'Fuck.' She moaned, grinding down as his hand rubbed across her pussy lips and his fingers found her clit, beginning to draw small circles around the sensitive nub.

'Still feeling those headaches?' She gasped, her fingers gripping onto his shoulders.

'It's going away.' He mumbled, his fingers leaving her clit and rubbing down her pussy, slipping two fingers into her, his thumb replacing them on her clit. 'You're so wet.'

Running out of patience, she reached down and unbuckled his belt and trousers, dragging his cock out, pulling a low moan from his lips. She wrapped her fingers around his cock, slowly beginning to pump him, drawing continuous moans from him. Her free hand weaved into his hair and she pressed her lips to his. Taking her hand away from his cock for a moment she moved her panties to the side, rubbing his cock along her folders, coating the tip in her own arousal. She pulled away from him to take a breath and slowly lowered herself onto his cock, both groaning as he filled her. She paused for a moment, using his shoulders to brace herself as she slowly began to bounce on his lap. He placed one hand on her hips and the other grabbed onto his desk, planting his feet firmly on the floor to stop anything from moving as his head fell back and a long moan escaped his lips. With the angle of his cock, she was coming apart quickly. He began to thrust his hips up, matching her movements, his cock hitting her g-spot with every thrust.

'I want you to cum around my cock.' He growled, holding her hips to stop her from moving as he began to thrust up into her, one of his hands slipping between their bodies, finding her clit and pressing down hard.

That made her fall apart, screaming out his name as she came. He continued to thrust up into her, chasing his own orgasm and dragging out hers until he came. She fell limp against his chest, panting. He wrapped his arms around her, trying to get his own breath back. He ran his fingers across her spine, the feeling soothing her.

'How is your headache?' She smiled.

'Gone.'

Beg

'Beg.' The words fell from his lips so easily, but so dangerously. His low voice cut through the silence. He has one thing on his mind. To make that word happen.

She knelt in the centre of the room, her hands laid out on her knees, her palms facing up. He circled her, his footsteps echoing on the wooden floor. She kept her eyes down, her breathing steady. He continued to circle her; the silence was deafening. She felt her stomach flipping whenever he disappeared from her vision. His voice cut through the silence again.

'How should I make you beg?' He asked, she wasn't allowed to speak. 'Should it be in pain? Or pleasure? Or I could just turn it on…' He whispered.

Her eyes went wide at the thought of it. Between her legs was a Sybian saddle – a vibrating bench that kept a dildo firmly lodged in her pussy. He held a remote in his hand, his thumb hovering over the 'on' button.

'How much would you beg with this on full? How much would I make you scream?' His voice was even lower, more dangerous.

He stopped in front of her, holding the remote to his side. He didn't say anything. Then she heard the 'click'.

A buzzing sound filled the room, with the Sybian on its highest setting, vibrating against her clit. She clenched her fists, the sensations overwhelming her. She squeezed her eyes shut to try and control herself.

'Palms up!' He commanded, her eyes snapped open and she forcibly relaxed her palms, laying them flat on her knees again.

It was the mark she saw before anything else. He was quick with the wooden cane, bringing it down across both of her palms. A white mark where the cane had met her skin, quickly turning her whole palm red as the pain blossomed in its wake. Going against her instincts, she fought against clenching her hands.

The soreness on her palms distracted her from the Sybian momentarily. But soon the overstimulation returned, feeling her whole body vibrate. It was all getting too much. To fast.

'Please, Sir can I come?' She squeezed her eyes shu trying to keep control.

He brought his hand to his face and slowly stroked h chin. 'Hmm, have you earned it?'

He grinned and she took a breath, her lips thinning into line. He knew the answer. She did too.

'Have you earned it?' He asked again, emphasizing eac word, waiting for his answer.

'No Sir.' Her voice trembled; she kept her eyes down.

'What was that?' He leaned down to her, holding th cane in her line of vision.

'I haven't earned it Sir,' she said louder, trying to stop he voice trembling.

'No, you haven't. You haven't been a good little slut.' H straightened himself, dropping the cane onto the floor with a lou crack.

He began to unzip his trousers, his erection twitchin against boxers. He flicked the switch on his remote and th

Sybian stopped vibrating. She fell forward as it stopped, bracing herself on the floor.

'Over here, now.' He growled. She quickly crawled over to him, resuming her position on her knees. He pushed his boxers down and freed his cock. His hands slowly stroked the hair out of her face. 'Now, earn that orgasm.'

She wasted no time, his cock pushing passed her lips to the back of her throat. Eager to please, she began to swirl her tongue around his length, hollowing her cheeks, listening to him moan.

His fingers weaved into her hair, gathering it up into a ponytail and using it as leverage. He began to snap his hips forward as she began to bob her head. Her eyes went wide when she felt him move, his shoe moving between her legs and the tip rubbing against her clit. Slowly she began to grind down on his shoe, the sensation building pleasure in her core. He began violently snap his hips into her, holding her head still as he thrust into her mouth. Tears fell from her eyes as she tried to breathe through her nose. It was sudden when she was pulled off and thrown onto the floor. She stayed there, gasping for gulps of air.

'Dirty fucking whore.' He growled, looking down at the wet patch on his shoe. 'Clean it.'

She quickly crawled over, kneeling in front of him and leaned down to his feet. He flicked up to his toe, watching as she began to lick her juices off his shoe. He smirked down at her, her tongue gliding across his shoe.

'I know you love this.' He growled. 'You're such a dirty whore.' He pulled his foot away and paused, staring down at her. She hadn't moved.

'Stand up and bend over, hands on your ankles.' He ordered, turning away from her.

She quickly stood and faced away from him, bending at her waist to grab her ankles, she widened her stance knowing what was coming.

She first felt his hands across her ass, gliding across the skin with ease. His hands slid down her legs to her pussy. His fingers running over her labia. She sealed her lips to stop a moan slipping through. He pinched her pussy lips then gently pulled them open. 'So, fucking wet.' He whispered, she could hear the smirk in his voice. 'You're such a fucking whore. Getting wet from rubbing against a dirty shoe.'

She didn't disagree. She couldn't. It was true. She was practically dripping down her legs. She let out a shriek when she felt the hand come down on her arse, her fingers digging into her ankles as the red mark blossomed on her skin.

'Nothing to say?' He taunted.

'I am a dirty slut Sir.' She mumbled, squealing when she felt another strike on her ass.

'What was that?'

'I am a dirty slut, Sir.' She repeated louder, feeling his soothing hand rubbing her ass.

'Good girl.'

He pressed the tip of his finger into her pussy, sliding the single digit in and crooked it. She let out a stuttered gasp, feeling him press onto her g-spot. He added a second finger and began to thrust, hitting the spot perfectly every time. She dug her fingers into her ankles, taking in ragged breaths, trying control the pleasure as it began to build.

A few small moans slipped past her lips, her legs beginning to shake. 'Please, Sir.' She moaned. 'Please can I cum?' As soon as she uttered the words, his fingers were gone. She let out a whine, feeling the pleasure slowly ebb away. She began to shake as she held herself, the position beginning to stiffen her muscles. She felt his hand on her hip, the tip of his cock pressing against her pussy.

'Have you been good?' He teased, rubbing the tip of his cock against her folds, coating it in her arousal.

'Yes, Sir.' She moaned.

'I suppose.' He hummed, pressing his cock further into her, it wasn't quite enough for pleasure.

'Please.'

'Please what?' He asked.

'Please fuck me, Sir.' She moaned. 'Please fuck me like the slut that I am.' She screamed when he pushed into her, sparing no mercy as began to thrust. He nearly pushed her over, his hands gripping onto her hips, so she couldn't fall. All she could do was hold her position as she felt the pleasure building. Ready to tip her over the edge, but not without asking first.

'FUCK.' She screamed. 'Please Sir can I cum?'

'Such a good fucking whore.' He growled, one of his hands running down her back. 'Cum for me.'

She didn't waste a second, letting the pleasure wash over her, her whole body shaking. He pulled out of her and let go of her hips. She immediately crumbled onto the floor, her limbs feeling numb. She lay on the floor, catching her breath as he began to pump his own cock, moaning as he came across her ass.

He smirked down at the view in front of him, then his gaze softening. 'You're beautiful.' He whispered, kneeling next to her. She slowly moved to rest her head in his lap as he gently rubbed her back.

'How are you feeling?'

'Amazing.' She hummed, curling into him like a cat. They sat in silence together, enjoying the end of the scene and the feeling of his hand rubbing her sore muscles.

This is bliss.

Mine

It was our girl's night out and I was supposed to b having a good time, but my brother had decided to appear at o bar, and with him, he had brought the man-whore who was h best friend.

I ignored him and continued my own night. We drank, w danced, but I couldn't help but glance over to the boys, m brother was lost in the crowd, but his friend was always in view. caught him staring at me once or twice. But who wouldn't, a blu ruffle mini dress made sure all the eyes were on me. I made m way back to the bar.

'Another glass!' I shouted, signalling the bartender befor I could put my money on the bar, another note was put down.

'I got this,' a male voice said, I hoped it would be him, bu turning I saw a stranger paying for my drink. 'Hi, I'm Nick.' H smiled. I took my drink from the bartender and smiled back.

'Hello.'

Girl's night or not, I spent the rest of the night with Nick. He tried to ply me with alcohol all night, but I kept to the soft drinks, keeping my head clear. We flirted, exchanged light touches, a caress of the hand, brushing intimately close to one another. Out of the corner of my eye, I could see Him watching us, every time I laughed, he would tense, and with every touch, I could see he was having to restrain himself. Nick was getting to him. Nick leaned close, his breath on the shell of my ear.

'Back to my place?' He asked. Grinning, I nodded and took his hand. Nick led us through the crowd and towards the door.

I was halfway to his car when some grabbed my wrist and tugged me backwards, after a few drinks and continued to stumble back into someone's hard chest. Looking up, I saw Him holding onto me. He looked pissed.

'What the hell?' Nick snapped.

'She's not going home with you.' He growled. 'Get lost.'

'What are you doing?' I snapped, pulling my wrist from his grip.

'Look, mate, she's old enough to make her own decisions, so why don't you let her?' Nick argued, holding out his hand to me, I smiled and reached out to him, but He tugged the wrist still in his hand and the slightest imbalance made me stumble.

'Get lost.' He warned. Nick and He stood glaring at one another before Nick scoffed.

'Bitch isn't worth it.' He said, walking back into the crowd.

'What were you thinking?" I shouted.

'I wasn't going to let you go home with that idiot.'

'Shouldn't you be with my brother?' I snapped, pulling my wrist from his grip.

'He went home with random chick hours ago.'

'Then why the hell are you still here?' I asked as he glanced back at me, licking his lips. Almost as if he was trying to figure out what to say.

'Come with me.'

'You're not my boyfriend. You don't make my decisions.' I tried to argue, but I still let him take my hand and pull me down an alleyway between the buildings.

'You shouldn't be going home with creeps like him.'

'I can go home with whoever I like.' I began to walk back to the bar, but he grabbed my wrist, pulling me backwards. Instead of speaking he pressed his lips to mine, one hand on my hip and the other on my shoulder. He pulled away, his lips barely touching mine.

'You're not going home with anyone.' He growled, he pressed his lips back to mine in a passionate, despite kiss. He pulled away from me for a moment.

'I want you to be mine.' He whispered; my lips parted as I realised everything I wanted was happening. I had it all. He didn't move for a moment, waiting for me to speak.

'Yes…' I breathed, it was all I could to him as he pressed me against the brick wall and his lips descending on my neck. Biting and kissing along my skin. I wrapped my arms around him, pulling him close to me, I could feel the hard-on through his jeans. Taking this as permission to continue, he grabbed my thighs and pulled me upwards. My dress riding up as I wrapped my legs around his waist.

His hands slowly wandered up to my thighs, pushing my dress up more and his fingers leaving a trail of fire on my skin. With his lips on my neck and his hands on my thighs, I couldn't think of anything else, I couldn't stop the moans from passing my lips. His hand reached down between us and pushed my panties to the side, his fingers moving up and down my pussy lips, already soaked from the teasing.

Smirking, he dropped my legs to the floor and grabbing my hips, spinning me to face the wall. He pulled my hips and ass out and I could hear him unzipping his trousers, I felt his chest as he leaned across my back, biting and sucking marks along my shoulders. Grabbing his cock, he ran the tip across my folds, and I pushed my hips backwards. He chuckled, one hand grabbing my hips and the other pushing his cock into me. A long moan slipped past my lips as I felt him stretching me. One of his hands ran up my back and over my shoulder, two fingers slipping into my mouth.

'Gotta keep you quiet.' He whispered as he began to thrust, his nails digging into my hips as his hit my ass. Moans continued to fall from my lips, the knot in my stomach tightening.

Nothing else mattered not the marks in my hips or the ones on my neck. The fingers in my mouth kept me quiet, but I just felt the need to cum. It wasn't long before the knot broke, pleasure washing over my whole body as my orgasm hit. My fingers clawed against the brick wall, my body tensing. He continued to thrust and came a few thrusts later, his hand tightening on my hip. There was a moment of silence before He slowly pulled out, helping to me to stand properly and sort myself out. I could feel his cum mixing with my arousal and dripping down my leg. He pulled down my dress and tucked himself back into his trousers, wrapping his jacket around my shoulders. He smiled and kissed my forehead.

'Come on.' He took my hand and led me out of the alley, walking towards his car.

Out of the alleyway, we saw Nick with a group of his own friends, hanging around his car with fast food. As we walked, I felt his hand move up my arm and to my neck, pulling the collar of his jacket down to make sure everyone could see all the hickies that were left there. Nick scowled at both of us.

Behind the Bar

The bar was slowly becoming empty as the morning drew in; the last few drunks had stumbled out and I could only see two people left, each nursing their drinks to the very last drop. I avoided eye contact, if they caught me, they would ask for more drinks. It was near closing time, but I'd still have to serve them and stay until they finished. Instead, I focused on cleaning up, putting all the clean glasses away, still warm from the industrial-sized dishwasher. I grabbed a rag and a spray bottle and began to wipe down the tables around the bar, hoping the last two customers would get the hint and leave.

I walked back behind the bar and dumped the bottle, wiping down the top of the bar absentmindedly. I heard the door open and my heart sank.

In the mirror behind the shelf, I watched the blurry figure become clearer, I couldn't stop the smile that rose up on my face. My boyfriend. He was normally on the day shifts. He ignored the other customers and walked around the bar. He wrapped his arms around my waist from behind, nuzzling his face into my shoulder, gently sway us.

'When do you finish?' He breathed into my skin.

'I can't leave until the last customer goes.' I whispered, glancing over to the last two men in the bar.

'But I was hoping to get you all to myself. Got things I need to do to you.' He whispered, pressing his hips against my ass. I smiled and pulled his arms from around my waist.

'I have to work.'

'Fine.' He shrugged, stepping away from me.

I expected him to leave and sulk until I got home – then I'd pay for it. But instead, he moved to stand in front of me and sunk down to his knees.

'What are you doing?' I gasped, feeling his fingers trail up my bare legs.

'You just carry on working; I'll enjoy myself down here.' He pushed my skirt up around my waist.

I gasped as I felt feather-light kisses along my thighs. His hand slipped between them and gently nudged them apart. His hands rubbed my skin, his fingers leaving a trail of fire behind him. He grabbed the hem of my panties and pulled them down my legs, they quickly dropped into his lap, stopping me from moving anywhere. Out of the corner of my eye, I could see the two drunks staring down at their drinks. They were not paying attention at all. I could feel my arousal building as his fingers trailed back up my legs, one hand stopping at my knee while the other grabbed my ass. With his hand on my knee, he lifted my leg, slowly guiding it to bend and rest on his shoulder. I gripped onto the bar for stability and he repositioned himself.

I didn't dare look down, trying to keep my cheeks from burning. He gently blew cold air onto my pussy, making me gasp, my knees almost giving way beneath me. I heard him chuckle. He wasted no time with teasing, instead, his fingers dug into my butt cheek as he pulled me forward and licked a long stripe across my pussy, eating me out as if I was his last meal. His tongue swirled, flicking my clit and driving me insane. My knuckles turned white as I gripped onto the bar. He paused for just a moment, looking up me.

'You're supposed to be working.' His lips glistened with my juices, but the smirk made me want to slap him.

'How am I supposed to be working?' I snapped, but it quickly trailed off into a moan as he dived back in. I released one hand from the bar and covered my mouth, the moans threatening to slip through my fingers.

I stared down at the counter, small whines slipping through my lips, I didn't dare lookup. The drunks were still nursing their drinks, but I was unsure whether they were wasted enough not to realise what was happening. I couldn't stop the moan escaping from my lips when I felt two fingers thrust up into me, his tongue focused on my clit as his fingers found their own rhythm.

I heard the door open and close once more, I could feel the heat rising from my chest to my cheeks. More customers? It was so close to closing now, I only had to survive a few more minutes.

'Still here?' The voice made both of us freeze. Looking up from the counter, our boss stood in the doorway, the two security guards from the door following closely behind. I tried to put my foot back on the floor, but he kept it up, his movements continuing.

'Y-Yes, Sir...' I squeaked; my breathing staggered as I tried to keep calm. The boss gave a nod to the security guards, in the direction of the last two customers.

'Close up and go home. I need you in an hour earlier tomorrow. We have a busy night.' He smiled. I nodded quickly hoping he would leave as I felt my end approaching.

The security guards took the drunks out of the bar, leaving just me, the boss, and him on the floor.

'You look very red, are you feeling okay?' The boss asked. Below me, he didn't stop thrusting his fingers or flicking his tongue against my clit.

'Fine,' I breathed. 'Absolutely fine.' I rushed the words out, trying not to moan.

'Very well.' He smiled, turning away and heading out the door. With a sigh of relief, I felt his fingers slow inside me, drawing out the orgasm for as long as he could. My legs began to shake, but I needed to stay upright until the boss was gone.

'Goodnight. I shall see you tomorrow.' He said as h grabbed one of the doors handles to close the doors, I raised m hand and waved, not daring to speak out loud.

He paused briefly and smiled at me.

'Oh, and by the way, tell your boyfriend he needs to clea up the floor once he's done down there.' I felt the heat rise fror my chest, my whole body turning red with embarrassment.

'Yes Sir!' His voice chimed in from the floor, the two me smiling at me as the boss closed the doors.

Finally, completely alone, I let myself fall, collapsing int his lap. He wrapped his arms around me, his lips and chin we with my orgasm.

'I hate you.' I sighed, leaning my head on his shoulde he chuckled, shaking his head.

'No, you don't.'

The git was right.

Interrogation

The handcuffs were tight on her wrists, the chain connecting her to the table making a loud noise as she angrily tugged at them. She had gotten caught in the city centre pickpocketing tourists.

Someone heard her struggles and walked into the interrogation room. A tall man sat across from her, a permanent scowl on his face, he dropped a file onto the table and took the chair opposite her.

'Miss Jones.' He spoke in a commanding voice and leaned back in the chair, folding his arms across his chest.

'What?' She snapped, the handcuffs creating angry red marks on her wrists.

'There is no need to be so hostile, Mss Jones. We simply want-' He could barely be heard over the sound of the chains.

'We just – will you stop that!' He grabbed her wrists and held them down on the table.

'We just want to ask you some questions.'

'The handcuffs don't give off that question time vibe.' She scoffed; the stranger chuckled his eyes quickly scanned over her body. The hair on the back of her neck stood on end as a shiver shot down her spine. He opened the file in front of her, pictures of bloody bodies attached. She winced at the pictures in front of her.

'The man we are looking for murdered of these three people.'

'What has that got to do with me?' She asked, trying not to look at the photos.

'CCTV shows you pickpocketing the suspect. All the information you have would be appreciated.'

She stared down at the photos and tried to remember, he gave her another blurry photo of her pickpocketing a man. She gave them everything she knew, once she had finished, she began to tug impatiently at the cuffs.

'Well?' She snapped, watching the smile curve up his lips. 'Are you going to let me go?' He lent back in his chair, crossing his arms over his chest.

'I don't know, I quite like you in handcuffs.'

She smirked, deciding to tempt him at his own games. 'It's not my favourite kink, but it's up there.'

His eyes went wide for a moment, his smug smile reappearing. 'I wonder what your other kinks are?' He stood and walked around the table, he was a tall man, as he walked around the table her face was level with his crotch, she could see his trousers becoming tight.

He moved to stand behind her, his fingers spreading across her shoulders. She shivered at his touch, a wave of arousal shooting down to her core. His fingers clenched around her shoulders and leaned down.

'Perhaps you could let me find out?' He whispered, his breath tickling her ear, she suppressed a moan.

'Perhaps you should.' She whispered back.

With the permission granted, his hands slid down her shoulders and down her chest, his fingers leaving a trail of fire as he reached her breasts, cupping one in each hand and beginning to massage them. She couldn't stop the moan that passed her lips this time, giving him a sign of approval. One hand disappeared from her beasts, moving back up to weave his fingers into her hair and yank her head back to see him.

'Hair pulling?' He smirked, his fingers gently massaging her scalp, she sucked in a breath.

'Yes Sir.' She gasped, his smirk grew, he let go of her hair, she fell onto the table.

'Pain and pleasure then.' He pulled the chair from beneath her, his hands grabbing her hips before she could fall, lifting her to stand and bend over the table, her wrists still cuffed to the middle.

'How high up this list am I?' He asked, his hands running down her back and over her ass.

His fingers dripped under her shirt, lifting her slightly and pushed it up over her head, bunching it up at the handcuffs, she gasped as her skin came into contact with the cold metal table, a sharp contrast to the trail of fire on her back. He did the same with her bra, bunching it up at the handcuffs and listening to her gasp as her nipples hardened against the table.

'Give me a clue.' He encouraged.

'Obedience.' She gasped out the words and she knew he had gotten the idea. A quick but hard smack came down on her ass. He grabbed her trousers unbuttoning the buttons and pulling them down over her ass, leaving them at her knees. Her underwear was a bright blue that couldn't be missed, he fingered the lace, flicking it against her skin, she flinched.

He lifted his hand again, bring it down in a sharp strike against her ass. She jolted forward, her hips hitting the edge of the table, she hissed in a mixture of pain and pleasure.

'How much do you think you could take?' He asked, his voice low and dangerous.

'More than you can give.' She smirked, seeing how far she could push him, his fingers were instantly woven into her hair and tugged her backwards, pushing his hips into her pressing his clothed cock against her ass. Her wrists tugged against the handcuffs, the harsh mix of pain and pleasure caused every movement she made to be followed by a moan, each one getting louder and louder as her pussy became wetter and wetter.

'Do you really want to test me?' He growled, over her shoulder, she could hear the metal of a buckle being undone followed by the rustle of trousers being pushed down. The trousers were abandoned on the floor, the blazer and tie he wore were stripped off and dumped them next to her on the table. His hands quickly moving back to her body, he grabbed her trousers and pushed them to her ankles, sweeping her feet and pulling them off completely.

'What are you doing?'

'I'm getting tired of you talking.' He mumbled, grabbing her panties and pulling them off as well. He leaned over her body, the tip of his cock pressing her ass. With his free hand he pushed to fingers into her mouth, she instantly reacted, swirling her tongue around his fingers, coating them in saliva, he pulled his fingers away but before she could close her mouth he shoved the panties in to gag her, his saliva coated fingers finding their way to her pussy, rubbing his fingers along her folds, the saliva mixing with her own juices.

'That's better.' He mused. 'Now all I get is your moans.' He continued to rub, his fingers flicking against her clit with every other stroke, making her hips buck backwards.

'How much can you beg with that gag.'

'Mmmmph. P-mph-ease.' She tried, but her words almost incoherent behind the gag.

He laughed. 'Adorable.' He pushed two fingers into her, crooking them upwards to hit her sweet spot, she cried out in pleasure and he continued. The pleasure almost tipped her over the edge, but her whole body jerked in shock as he pulled out.

'Mmmmph. P-mmph-lease.' She begged, desperately trying to do anything to stop the pleasure from slipping away.

'Such a needy little bitch.' He growled, grabbing her hips and holding her still, his other hand grabbing his cock and rubbing it along her folds, coating the tip in her juices. She continued to moan a muffle variation of 'please'. It wasn't enough.

A low growl slipped past his lips and he pushed into her, forcing his entire cock balls-deep into her. His girth stretching her and making her cry out. He didn't spare a moment, wrapping his forearm around her waist to stop her hips from hitting the table, but it didn't stop the feeling of his pelvis slapping against her ass, the pleasure began to mount up again. Each thrust adding more pain and pleasure to her body, each thrust building further towards her orgasm. While holding her in the air he positioned her at an angle, so that his cock was angled perfectly towards her g-spot.

She cried out in pleasure, her orgasm building more and more until she was ready to break. He leaned over her and pulled the panties out of her mouth.

'Don't you dare cum without begging.' He growled.

'Please. Please. PLEASE! Let me cum!' She was almost in tears; the pleasure was too much.

'Cum for me, you little bitch.' He whispered into her ear. She didn't need telling twice. She let everything go, screaming out as her orgasm racked through her body. Every muscle shaking and her pussy walls clenching around his cock. His orgasm followed a few thrusts later, holding her hips flush against his pelvis as he shot streams of cum into her. Once they were both satisfied, he pulled out of her and gently put her feet back to the ground. He pulled the chair back beneath her and lowered her onto the seat, watching her flinch as her red ass met the cold metal of the chair.

He ran his fingers over her skin in a soothing manner, as she caught her breath again, a mixture of both they're cum dripping out of her onto the chair. He pulled his trousers back on in silence, redoing his tie and putting on his blazer. He collected the files that had been spread across the opposite end of the table, smiling at her.

'How far up this kink list did I get?' He asked.

'Pretty high.' She breathed.

'Many I could keep finding those kinks in future.'

'Definitely.' She laughed, but her smile quickly dropped as he walked towards the door. 'Wait! Aren't you going to let me out?'

He pulled the handle of the door turning back to her with a smirk across his lips. 'You're a pickpocket, you should easily to pick the lock on handcuffs.'

'WHAT THE FUCK!'

Good Grades

She ran her fingers along the visitor's pass that wa
clipped to her skirt, watching as elevator lit up each floor
passed. She shifted her balance from foot to foot, eager to se
him. Her gaze shifted from the numbers to the door, hoping that
wouldn't stop on any other floors. She moved her hand to he
satchel, all her work safely inside it. Her evening class ha
finished, and she had picked up her assignment today. The grad
wasn't anywhere near what she expected, but it was the firs
assignment in the semester, she knew she'd get better. It wou
just take some improvement.

The elevator dinged on her floor and she quickly exited
pulling the bag back onto her shoulder as her heels clicke
against the laminate flooring. She ignored the glances from th
men in the cubicles, heading straight for the office she needed
even a few women turned their heads as she walked. When sh
reached the door she gently rapped on the wood, glancing ove
her shoulder to see the men leaning out of their cubicles to stare

the women were staring daggers at their own computers. She shifted her weight from foot to foot as she waited.

Eventually, the door opened, his smiling face greeting her.

'Hello, beautiful.' He grabbed her hand and pulled her into the office, shutting the door behind him. He wrapped his hand around her waist and pressed a quick kiss to her lips, leading her back to the desk. She dumped her satchel on top of all his paperwork. He sat back at his desk and pulled her down with him, sitting her comfortably on his lap. His hand slipped beneath her shirt and rested on her back, his fingers rubbing small circles on her skin. She leaned into him, the office aircon was not the only thing leaving goose bumps on her skin. His fingers were as light as feathers, gliding gently across her bare leg.

Her breath hitched as his fingers went higher, reaching the hem of her skirt before stopping.

'How are the evening classes?' He asked.

'They are hard.' She sighed, staring down at his fingers, still on her leg, unmoving. 'I got my first assignment back today.'

She leaned closer, letting her hand fall onto his wrist, hoping to encourage him. His hand didn't move, instead, the hand that rested on her back moved away and reached for her satchel. She barely noticed as she leaned her head on his shoulder, feeling his fingers beginning to move in small circles. Her eyes slowly closed, enjoying the feeling of his hand on her. Meanwhile, he expertly opened her satchel with one hand and pulled out the papers she had in there. The typed-up pages where all stapled together, the one on the top covered with red pen marks and a large letter grade in a circle at the top.

'A D?' He asked, bringing her attention back.

'What?' She mumbled.

'You got a D.'

'It was the first assignment. It will get better.' She shrugged.

He turned her off his lap and made her stand.

'You are so smart. Why didn't you get an A?' he asked.

'It was the first assignment.' She repeated.

His hand spread across her back and pushed her down, bending her over the table across the desk. 'That's not an answer.' He whispered, his hand moving down across her skirt.

'I rushed it.' She admitted, feeling his fingers grab her skirt, slowly pulling it down her legs. She could feel her excitement the moment his hands touched her bare skin.

'Why did you rush?' he asked, his fingers rubbing ass.

'I didn't start it until late. I didn't have the time.' She gasped. His fingers inched closer to her pussy, brushing against her bikini line.

'Why didn't you start earlier?'

'Why do you need to ask all the questions?' She moaned, squealing when he suddenly flicked her clit, a wave pleasure shooting through her.

'Answer the question.' His voice was low.

'I was putting it off until I absolutely had to. Anxiety and all that.'

His fingers remained on her clit, rubbing slow circles as she moaned. The pleasure slowly built as she bucked her hips backwards. His other hand kept her hips still as he easily slid two fingers inside her. She gasped as she felt his fingers stretching her.

'Why didn't you talk to me?' He asked, slowly moving his fingers and thumb in sync.

'I... I...' She moaned, her words quickly turning into moans, she couldn't finish a sentence.

'Why didn't you talk to me?' He asked again, his fingers slowing to a stop.

'I wanted to do it on my own.' She blurted, bucking her hips backwards to create her own movement. He slowly started moving again.

'You don't have to do things on your own.' He began to move his fingers faster. 'You know you can lean on me whenever you need.'

The pleasure kept building as he thrust his fingers into her. She was so close. So close and then he pulled out. She gasped and whined as he did, pulling up her underwear and skirt.

'WHAT THE FUCK?!' She shouted.

He pulled her back into his lap and pressed a kiss to her cheek. 'Your next assignment is due next week. Get an A. We'll finish this then.' He smirked.

'What... What do you mean?' She stuttered, he pushed all her papers back into her bag and handed it to her.

'I've got work to do.' He smiled.

She stuttered as he pushed her out of the office, leaning in close to her.

'No finishing yourself off.' he warned. 'I'll see you tonight?'

'But...But...'

'Nice dinner?' He whispered, his breath tickling the shell of her ear. 'I want to see that A.'

Forgive Me, Father, for I Have Sinned

The wooden pew was hard against her ass, it was uncomfortable and cold, and it didn't help the ache she felt whenever she entered the church, she needed to change her underwear after each service. She would always get there earlier than the rest, hoping to get some time alone with him. He had only come to the church a few months ago, but since he had arrived, the congregation had doubled. She had never been very religious, but as soon as she saw him, it tempted her. A priest she could ruin.

She took her seat in the front pew, absentmindedly looking around,, passing the time by counting the many different things in the church. Frequently glancing at the oak patterned boxes to the side of her. She waited for the familiar click of the door unlatching, but it seemed to take forever. She squeezed her thighs together, the thought of what would happen in those boxes sending a wave of heat between her thighs.

When the familiar click finally came, she almost jumped out of her skin with excitement. It was a whole hour before the next service, and no one was waiting in line. She had a full hour. An elderly woman stepped out of the box, her cane echoing as it hit the wooden floor of the church. The priest opened the other door, quick to help her. They passed a few quiet words between them and the old women slowly left the church. He was young and slim, a small bit of stubble across his face which was usual for him, but it made it look older. He was handsome, she could only imagine what was under the black shirt, it was intentionally lost, but she was sure there was a chiselled chest beneath.

He finally noticed her sitting in the pew, his classic smile dropped, and he took in a breath, his eyes scanning her body and his cock twitched in his trousers.

Her top is too low. Her skirt is too short. I shouldn't... He had wondered what she always did there, dressed modestly, but also managing to show just enough skin to make his trousers uncomfortably tight.

'Did you want confession?' He asked, skipping all the politeness, he needed to get back into the box where he was safe, no one could see him and there was a wall of wood between them.

'Yes please.' Her voice was delicate but held secrets. He gestured her to follow and he opened the confessional box door to her, she stepped in silently, her hand gliding over his on the handle. He quickly shut the door behind her, running into the box next to her.

He took a moment to compose himself, and pulled back the small wooden divide, spotting her auburn hair as she stared down at her lap.

'Forgive me Father for I have sinned.' She whispered, there was silence for a moment, the priest couldn't help but think what perhaps these sins could be, he had to ask.

'What are your sins?' He kept his voice low, only serving to give her more ideas.

'I have ungodly thoughts, Father, of a man.' She spoke quietly as if someone outside might hear her. But the words caught the priest, he needed to ask.

'Thoughts?'

'Yes, Father, thoughts of man. In my mind this man, he is touching me.'

'Touching you?' he urged her to continue, the thoughts stirring his cock.

'Yes, I can feel his hands on me. I can feel them, gliding across my skin.' As she spoke, she dragged her hands up her own thighs, pushing the material of her skirt up.

'T-touching you where?' His voice shook, he could feel his cock straining against his trousers,

'Well, at first he starts with his hands on my hips, then he slowly slides down my body, over my ass, down my thighs to my knees, just to bend them upwards and spread them how he wants to.'

A sudden slam of the door cut her sentence short. *Had he gone?* Had he rushed out? Had she finally broken the priest? Her thoughts were cut short when the door was yanked open, the priest staring back at her, his once nearly combed hair ruffled, and his belt half undone.

'Get out.' He growled, his eyes staring at her with hunger, with lust.

Father, I-' She couldn't finish her sentence as the priest grabbed her arm and dragged her out of the confessional. He pulled her forward, not towards the door, but his office.

He practically threw her into the room, slamming the door behind him.

'Who is on your mind?' He snapped, his eyes scanning over her entire body, she smirked at him, taking a sultry step towards him.

'There is only one man on my mind, Father.' She whispered, continuing to walk forward until she stood directly in front of him.

'Who.' He growled.

'Forgive me, Father, for I have sinned.' She whispered, sinking down to her knees. 'I have had ungodly thoughts of a man. Of a man of God.' The priest did nothing as she knelt in front of him, finishing the unbuckling that he had begun. The belt and trousers easily came loose.

'I have had thoughts of him touching me, of me touching him, of us both enjoying the pleasure of each other's bodies.' She watched for any sign of reluctance, but he stared down at her with desire. His cock jerked against his boxers. She smiled when she felt his hands caress her, slowly moving to her wrists.

'Who is this man?' He asked, his voice low as he wrapped his fingers around her wrists.

'He is a man of God, Father, a Reverend in a church.' He moved her wrists away from him, for a moment she thought he wanted to stop, but then he spoke.

'Then you must be punished, my dear, for fantasizing about a man of God is a definite sin.'

She looked up as saw a smirk across his lips. 'Anything Father.' She smiled; he pulled her hands forward to the hem of his boxers.

'You must repent your sins. Cleanse yourself of these impure thoughts.' His fingers left her wrists and glided up her arms, leaving a trail of fire as she slowly pulled his boxers and trousers down together, his cock finally bouncing free.

'Cleanse yourself.' He whispered, his fingers leaving her skin to weave into her hair, holding it out of her face. She didn't need any encouragement, holding onto his hips to keep herself steady, she took his tip into her mouth, swirling her tongue around it. The priest let out a low moan. She began to bob her head, taking more and more of him into her mouth until she was almost at the base. She forced back her gag reflex as her nose pressed against his pelvis, the priest let out a moan and held her head still, his cock filling her mouth and cutting off her airway. He released her after a few seconds and she pulled back, losing her balance and falling onto the floor as she took in a breath, saliva coated her lips as she smiled up at him.

He grabbed her wrists and dragged her to stand.

'Bend over the desk.' He whispered to her. 'Every aspect of your filthy body must be cleansed.' Hearing such words from that man sent a wave of heat right to her core. She quickly obeyed, bending over the desk and trying not to lie on anything that would hurt her, the old wood was cold against her chest, her nipples grew pert against her bra and shirt.

She felt the priest's hands against her back, slowly feeling down her body and over her ass, grabbing the hem of her skirt at her knees and pulling it up over her ass.

'You need to be cleansed of all your sins.' He whispered pulling her panties down her legs, kneeling behind her.

'Forgive me Father, for I have sinned.' She whispered, feeling his hands on her bare ass, massaging the cheeks. She cried out in ecstasy when she felt his tongue against her pussy, flicking her clit. She held onto the edge of the table, her hips bucking backwards, and his fingers began to dip into her hole. She moaned and let her desire take over, her hips bucking backwards as his fingers slipped into her, stretching her open.

'Fuck. Oh god.' Her moan turned into a yelp when he delivered a swift slap to her ass.

'Blasphemy? You are really are a dirty girl.' He whispered, he stood up and wrapped his hand around his cock, pumping it a few times. 'We need to cleanse you properly.' With one hand on his cock, he grabbed her hip and guided her backwards, the tip of his cock pressing against her hole. He pushed his hips forward, thrusting into her to the hilt, his pelvis pressing against her ass. She cried out as he stretched her, he only paused for a moment until he pulled out so only the tip was inside her, before thrusting back into her and continuing at a wild pace, his fingers digging into her hips as he held her still. She reached down her body, her own fingers tapping against the clit, rubbing in a small circle and sending her over the edge. She cried out as she came, her walls clenching around his cock, holding him still and dreading his own orgasm from him a few thrusts later.

He pulled out of her, falling onto a chair behind them. His cum mixed with her juices and began to drip down her leg. Slowly, she slipped off the desk, falling to her knees on the floor. The cum pooling on the floor beneath her. She smiled breathlessly over her shoulder, watching the priest tuck himself back into his trousers. He fixed his appearance and readjusted his dog collar.

'The service starts soon.' He smirked, he walked past her to the other side of the table.

'Some old woman left these from my last meeting. They should keep you still for a while, let's hope for your sake she doesn't come back here to look for them.' He said as he walked back around the desk. She looked up at him confused until he wrapped the rosary beads tightly around her wrists and then wrapped the other end around the table leg, securing her to the floor with her skirt bunched up at her waist and her panties around her ankles.

'What are you doing?' She snapped; he pressed a kiss to her forehead.

'You still have sins to cleanse. I'll be back later.'

The Dinner Party

Her stomach dropped as she walked into the room. It was full of guests. The women wore elegant lace masks over their eyes while the men wore what looked like plastic over theirs. The room was loud, everyone ignored her, she received a few glances, but a naked girl carrying a tray was nothing new in that place.

She swallowed, as her throat moved, she felt the soft leather against her skin, calming her nerves slightly. He was here. She was safe. She took a step forward, her heels clicking on the floor, but that wasn't what caught the attention of the guests, it was the chains. The delicate silver chains around her wrists rattled together against the tray she held. The chains came up between her breasts and looped through the small metal ring on the leather collar, ensuring she could never straighten her arms without feeling the tug against her neck.

She wandered around the party, people taking glass flutes of champagne and replacing them with their empty ones. She wouldn't dare look the guests in the eye, she kept her head down, focusing on walking in the new shiny stilettos he had brought her. Whether it was a gift or torture she'd never know. The brand-new shoes pinched her toes, but they were so pretty, too pretty to scuff or mark, too dangerous too. When her tray was full of empty glasses, she headed back to the table to replace and refill. It was all she had to do.

As she was filling new glasses, she felt everyone's eyes on her, staring at her ass bent over the table as they walked past her. As she filled the last glass, she found a familiar scent, calming her nerves and igniting her senses. His hands were on her ass before he spoke, warm hands caressing her skin.

'You better not spill anything.' He whispered; she could almost hear a smirk.

'I won't Sir.' She whispered, straightening her back with the tray in her hand she turned to him, the only person who she could look in the eye when he allowed her too.

'Good girl.' He murmured, his hand still on her ass. She waited for his hand to move until she began to walk, feeling his eyes on her as she walked away, swaying her hips more as she did.

She could always see him out of the corner of her eye as she served. His presence did many things for her. He made her feel safe and calm, always being around. But it also made her suspicious. His eyes constantly on her, like an animal stalking its prey. The thought of him pouncing on her sent shivers down her spine.

'Stay here.' A voice instructed her, the man was hidden behind the mask, talking to a small group of people. She stayed still, holding the tray out for them as they drank each flute.

They're going to get kicked out if they're too drunk.

Keeping her eyes down, she scanned the rest of the party, taking in what she could with her restricted gaze. Looking around, she didn't notice him until he was standing right next to her.

'Excuse me, gentleman.' He smiled, using all his charm. I am afraid I must steal her away from you.' No one argued as the hand on her back slowly pushed her forward. Once away from the small crowd his hand disappeared from her back, taking the tray off her and placing it on a nearby table. He grabbed the chain near the metal ring and dragged her forward, she almost tripped in her stilettos as she tried to keep up with him.

He pointed to a small bench. 'On your back.'

She quickly complied. It was only wide enough to comfortably rest her back against the cushion. He lifted her legs and pressed a finger softly into the back of her knee, giving the signal to bend. He reached into his pocket and pulled out some more silver chain, looping it around each ankle and threading it through the metal ring. Her hands grabbed her knees, trying to keep the position.

He pushed her legs open and smiled. She looked nervous.

'Don't move.' He warned as he walked away. She stayed still, staring at the ceiling and listening for footsteps.

He returned moments later with a small box, placing it on the floor next to the bench.

'Safe word?' He asked.

'Cucumber.' She smiled up at him. He returned her smile before reaching into the box, pulling out his first implement. she knew what it was as soon as she heard the clicking of another chain. His hands moved across her chest and to her nipples, pinching them hard enough for her to let out a small whine.

'It's only going to get worse.' He smirked, pinching on the nipple and attaching the clamp, her lips thinned as she tried to hold in the sound. But he wasn't happy. He attached the other clamp and gently tugged on the chain.

FUCK FUCK FUCK.

He pulled the chain to her lips.

'Open.' He commanded; her lips parted as he put the chain between her teeth. 'Let go and you'll be in trouble.' The chain between her lips gave a constant tug on her nipples, she could already feel them going numb, she whined. 'Complain and I'll put them somewhere else.'

Her eyes widened, and she silenced herself. He continued to smirk way too much.

Smug bastard.

Once he was satisfied, he took the box and moved to stand at her feet, watching her arousal began to drip down her ass. His fingers ghosted over her skin, lightly tickling her, but making her want more. It was the way he liked it, remaining fully dressed while she was naked and powerless. He easily pushed her body up the bench slightly, her head dropping off the edge. For more than one reason. She couldn't see anything he was doing. She could only watch the party go on upside down as the blood rushed to her head, more tugging on the clamps.

He loved playing these games. No matter how many times he would do it, she would never be prepared for the next one, and she would never see it coming. He had volunteered her for the party, promising rewards later. Hopefully, this was leading to a reward.

A light buzzing sound excited her. She knew exactly what that was. Fully charged she hoped. She didn't expect it to be pressed directly on her clit, it made her jolt. She jumped up and looked down her body, between the valley of her breasts she could see the bright purple vibrator being pressed against her clit.

She looked up at him and he pressed a finger to her lips, knowing she wanted to talk, to scream, to moan.

She clamped her teeth hard around the chain, trying not to speak. She was so focused on being silent she didn't even notice the pinwheel come out until she felt the spiked wheel being pulled across her skin. The love-hate relationship with implement was there. He loved it and she hated it. But it had the effect they both wanted. The combination of the vibrator and the wheel was a new kind of heaven she wasn't sure if she liked.

She felt the pleasure building, the pinwheel kept it from spilling over. He removed the vibrator and the pinwheel together, leaving her wanting and needing. His hand waved over her, but the gesture wasn't for her. A man appeared in front of her, her head level with his crotch. Her heart began to race. They had spoken about this before.

But was he going ahead with it now?

The stranger looked down at her, giving her a warm smile. His hand crawled up her abdomen as the stranger shrugged off his jacket.

'She is well behaved, best blow job here by far.' He smiled, the stranger smirked back at him, looking down at her. 'Would you like to try?'

'Safe word.' The stranger asked, looking down at her.

'Cucumber.' She replied, her words muffled as she kept hold of the chain.

'You can let go now,' he said, and she quickly dropped the chain from her teeth, the pain on her nipples only lessening a fraction.

'Safe gesture?' The stranger asked, she quickly put three fingers up as high as she could in the chains. They both nodded to one another.

She watched at the stranger unbuckled his trousers, a silent agreement between them both had been conducted, she was just the goods. He pushed his trousers down to mid-thigh, his cock bouncing free.

'Let's see how good you really are.' The stranger said. The tip of his cock ran across her lips as she opened her mouth, and the stranger slid it in. She kept her head still as the stranger began to thrust into her, his hands either side of his jaw. At the other end, she felt his fingers began to glide across her ass and

thighs, getting so close to where she wanted them, but not close

enough. The stranger moaned above her, his hand stroking her

jaw as he pushed deeper and deeper. Her gag reflex had been

trained away; she didn't even flinch when the tip hit the back of

her throat. She instead focused on the other pair of hands, finally

reaching her pussy. She recognized the hands, his hands.

He wouldn't let a stranger put their hands down there,

touching was his. A muffled moan passed her lips as he began to

run his fingers along her pussy lips, his finger quickly being

coated in her juices before he pushed it into her entrance, his

thumb rubbing her clit as he thrust the finger in and out of her.

As the stranger thrust his cock into her mouth, his finger

crossed her throat, feeling the bulge as the cock pushed further

down her throat, the stranger moaned and gripped onto the table

At the other end, she could feel his fingers thrusting into

her, making her back arch of the table as his thumbs rubbed her

clit.

They were soon gone though. She wanted to look up and

shout, but all she could do was whine and clench her pelvis

trying to feel something down there. Someone's hands began to grab at her breasts, pinching and squeezing the tender flesh. The moans dripped freely from her lips, muffled by the cock. She almost screamed when she felt it. Another cock pushing into her, the familiarity of him inside her, his hands holding onto her thighs as he began to thrust. Her back almost arched off the table, but the two sets of hands on her kept her still. She wanted to writhe and moan, but she could do nothing. Being used for the pleasure of the two men that surrounded her.

Deliciously wrong.

The stranger's cock began to twitch, his end coming soon. She tried to focus on the stranger by hollowing her cheeks, but His thumb began to draw circles on her clit as he thrust, her mind going blank. Her own pleasure built as the two men used her for their satisfaction. Eventually, the stranger pulled out of her, pumping his cock in his hand a few times before letting out an animalistic grunt and cumming, shooting his seed across her chin and down her chest, gripping onto the table to steady himself. He sighed and gently stroked her jaw.

'Fucking amazing.' He whispered as he tucked himself back into his   trousers.

I barely did anything.

'How does it feel to be used for someone else's pleasure? Such a good slut.' The stranger whispered in her ear. At the other end, He was chasing his own orgasm, the stranger was finished and now just enjoying the show that he had a personal invite to. The stranger's hand weaved into her hair, holding her head up to watch the man at the other end as his cock disappeared into her pussy.

He pressed his thumb to her clit, rubbing harsh circles on it.

'Fuck.' He growled, thrusting into her a few more times before pulling out and pumping his cock with his hand, his cum shooting across her stomach. He was breathing heavily, smiling down at her. The stranger let go of her hair resting her head back. The stranger shook his hand and they chatted for a moment, she barely listened. The stranger walked away from her, joining the main crowd again, and He turned back to her.

Her orgasm was so close, yet now, as she lay untouched, she could feel it slipping away. Standing beside the side of her, His eyes raked over her body.

'Do you want something?' He asked teasingly, she quickly nodded.

'Please, Sir.' She whined.

'What is it that you want?' He asked, moving to stand at her legs again. He knew the answer.

'Please Sir, I want to cum.' She whispered, craning her neck to watch his movements. He pulled out the vibrator again.

'Do you want this?' He flicked the switch and held it teasingly close to her clit.

'Oh fuck... Yes, please Sir...' She begged.

'Well, since you've been good.' He flicked the vibrator onto its highest setting and pressed it against her clit. Her back instantly arched, not caring anymore as she chased her own orgasm. He pushed two fingers into her, moving his body to the side and crooking his fingers to find the sweet spot he knew all too well. Her vision went white.

Her whole body began to shake, pleasure took over her as he cried out, arching so much she almost fell off the table. He held her still as she came, removing his fingers and the vibrator as she came down from her high. Her whole body was numb. He quickly undid the chains and let her legs fall, hanging off the table.

While the party went on, he removed all the chains from her body, leaving the collar in place and pulling another table next to her to lie her head-on. His fingers were gentle on her skin as everything was placed back into the box. He leaned down and gently stroked her hair, pressing a kiss to her forehead.

'Five minutes.' He whispered. 'Then get yourself cleaned up. The guests have requests.' He smiled, looking over to the rest of the party she could see some people watched them. She smiled and whispered.

'Yes, Sir.'

'Good girl, you're not going to disappoint anyone.'

If every request was like this one, no one is going to be disappointed.

The Lawyer & The Doctor

I flicked through the papers on my desk, all the information was in front of me for the new client. The court case was to begin in a week and I still needed to speak to the doctor and his lawyer. Thankfully they were old friends and both coming to my office to discuss the case. I had never met either of them, but they were both regulars in the courthouse, and apparently very handsome.

The knock at my door brought my attention back to the present.

'Come in.' I called. A man in a white coat entered followed by a man in a suit. Both of them were handsome, chiselled jawlines and bright eyes.

'Do you normally walk around in scrubs?' I asked the doctor.

He smirked at me as he sat down in the chair opposi'
my desk. 'It makes it easier to pick up ladies.'

'I'd be careful about picking up women in
courthouse. You never know what they've done.' I smiled back
him

The lawyer chuckled. 'I told you I wasn't the only one wh
thought so.'

'So, you are the lawyer for the defendant?' I asked hin
The lawyer smiled and nodded as I turned to the doctor.

'And your one who examined her after the assault?'

The doctor sat up in his chair and his smile dropped
'Yes.'

The meeting lasted over two hours discussing the detail
of the case, the day had ended by the time we had finished.

'Can I interest you in a drink?' The lawyer asked as w
left my office together. I sighed, my mind was telling me to g
home and prepare the case. But I couldn't pass up th
opportunity to drink with two handsome men.

We ended up in a bar close to my office. The lawyer headed over to the counter while the doctor and I found a place to sit.

'So, tell me the truth,' the doctor said, 'the attraction, it isn't just one way is it?'

I felt the heat rising on my cheeks. 'W-What?'

'You're attracted to me? And to my friend of course.' He said.

I laughed and shook my head. 'You've had to get me pretty liquored up before I answer questions like that.' Just as I spoke, the lawyer returned holding a tray of shots.

'She wants liquor before she answers the question.' The doctor laughed and the lawyer fell into the seat next to me, dropping his arm over the back of my seat.

'Well, that means a yes doesn't it?' The lawyer laughed.

I could feel my cheeks reddening with every word.

'Are you worried about having to choose between us?' The doctor asked.

I quickly picked up a shot and downed it, not wanting to answer the question. He wasn't wrong.

'Why do you have to?' The lawyer asked, and I almost choked.

'What?'

'Why do you have to choose?' The lawyer repeated. 'You see, we made a deal when we were in high school. We don't fight over girls. If they're willing, we share.'

'Share?' I repeated, I couldn't believe what I was hearing. I also couldn't believe how much the conversation appealed to me.

'We share. We both get the fun, and the girl gets the best time of her life.' The doctor smirked.

'You just need to say yes.' The lawyer added. I took in a shaky breath, was I really going to say yes to this? I couldn't believe it as the words passed my lips.

'Yes.'

The lawyer and the doctor smirked at me, each grabbing my hand and pulling me back up.

'Wait! What about the shots?' I asked.

'They're just water.' The lawyer shrugged. 'Can't have you too drunk to make good decisions.' He smirked. We all clambered into a taxi, the lawyer gave the driver an address.

'What would have happened if I had said no?' I asked.

'Then you'd be missing out.' The doctor smirked, turning me to face him and pressing a kiss to my lips. I wasn't sure whose it was, but a pair of hands moved up my legs, gently squeezing my thigh.

The hotel came a little too quickly. Stuck between both men as they lead me up the hotel room. Once inside they began to unbutton their shirts.

'Strip for us.' The lawyer smiled. Both men's clothes quickly piled on the floor, down to just their underwear. I quickly followed and stripped, piling my clothes on the floor and I faced the doctor as he sat down on the bed.

The lawyer stood behind me, my back flush against his chiselled chest. His fingers brushed up against my arm, slowly leaving a trail of fire as they moved across my skin, up my arm and over my shoulder. His hand eventually settling on my throat, squeezing ever so gently and making my breath hitch. I felt his breath   on   my   ear.

'I would say to be nice, but she seems to be enjoying it.' The doctor smiled, watching her body twitch as the lawyer tightened and relaxed his grip on her throat. The lawyer's other hand gently glided across my stomach and down to my pussy. His fingers lazily tapped my clit, small moans slipping past my lips. I could see the Doctor opposite me, pumping his own erection. I could feel my legs beginning to shake, even the lightest touch on my clit was sending me into a frenzy.

The lawyer suddenly pulled away from me. A small whine passed my lips before I even thought about it. I could see the lawyer smirk as he walked around me, his eyes scanning my body. 'Onto the bed. On your hands and knees.' He ordered.

I quickly complied, climbing onto the bed and facing the headboard.

'Would you prefer the back or the front?' I heard the lawyer ask.

There was a slight pause before I heard the doctor. 'Her mouth has been particularly inviting.' There was a small chuckle shared between the two men before they got into their positions.

The doctor climbed up onto the bed, standing on the mattress so that his cock was level with my lips. The lawyer knelt behind me, his fingers finding my clit once more.

'Open.' The doctor held the base of his cock, rubbing the tip against my lips until I opened, flicking my tongue against him. I took the tip into my mouth, slowly bobbing my head to take more and more until his cock hit the back of my throat.

'Fuck.' He moaned, bucking his hips forward. I forced my gag reflex back as his fingers weaved into my hair and he began to control my movements.

Behind me the lawyer continued to rub my clit, two of his fingers easily slipping into my cunt. I felt his other hand rubbing across my ass as he began to pump his fingers. I moaned around the doctor's cock, trying to focus on the task in front of me. But the Lawyer moved his fingers faster, his thumb hard against my clit. Everything around me started to buzz, the pleasure mounting.

I cried out as I came, his fingers thrusting inside to drag it out for as long as possible. My legs trembled as I tried to keep my position. The lawyer grabbed my hips, pulling me off the doctor's cock. Pulling his fingers out of me, the lawyer reache

forward and slipped his fingers into my mouth. In an orgasm

haze, I swirled my tongue around his fingers, greedily lapping u

everything until he pulled out again. 'Greedy.' He mused as h

kissed my shoulder. 'Now we've pleasured you, you need

return the favour.' He whispered, gently pulling me backwards.

I followed his movements, settling on the edge of the be

as the doctor lay down on the mattress. The lawyer leaned clos

to my ear.

'Ride him.' On Shaky legs, I crawled up the doctor's body

resting my knees either side of his hips. He held the base of hi

cock, rubbing it against my folds and coating the head in m

juices. Slowly, I sunk down onto him, a moan slipping past m

lips as I felt him stretch me. Bracing my hands on his chest

slowly began to roll my hips, the doctor's head falling back in

moan.

I felt a hand gently rest on my back. The lawyer slowl

pushed me forward until my chest was pressed against th

doctor's. Behind me, I felt the lawyer's fingers move downwards still coated in my saliva and juices as he pressed a single digital against my asshole. I forced myself to relax.

'You don't mind we use this end too, do you?' The lawyer smirked, pushing his finger further, gently thrusting.

'Fuck no.' I whispered, beginning to buck my hips backwards. His continued to thrust his finger, slowly adding a second. A moan slipped past my lips as he continued to move, my own juices dripping down my thighs.

I looked down at the doctor beneath me, his hands gently moving up my sides and cupping my breasts. Gently massaging them, he began to pinch my nipples, I flinched and arched my back, the motion moving the lawyer's fingers and hitting the right spot. I cried out in pleasure as he continued to thrust his fingers into the same spot, the pleasure mounting more and more.

The doctor pinched my nipples harder; I jerked my hips down further onto his cock, the lawyer's fingers following. The doctor began to thrust his hips upwards, the combination of his hips and the lawyer's fingers sending waves of pleasure through my body.

The lawyer's fingers left my asshole and the doctor paused. My whole body trembled as the bed dipped behind me. The lawyer's knees sat parallel with mine, his cock pressing against my back entrance. I felt his hand drift up to my spine, leaving goose bumps across my skin. The lawyer slowly pushed into me, and the doctor's hands moved to my clit and rubbing fast circles, taking my mind away as the cock pushed into me. It was considerably larger than his two fingers as the lawyer slowly pushed past my rim, his hands securely on my shoulders as he pulled me back onto his cock.

He went slow, as the he pulled me back, I moved down, eventually feeling both men's pelvises against my ass and thighs. Everything paused, both men enjoying the feeling of being inside me while allowing me to get used to the feeling.

'Fuck. The doctor uttered beneath me. Together, they began to move. One pulled out as the other pushed in. Creating the perfect rhythm to send shockwaves through my body.

I couldn't hold myself together, the pleasure made my whole-body shake, my arms trembling so much they gave way beneath me, I fell onto the doctor's chest, creating a whole new angle as the lawyer grabbed my hips, thrusting deeper into me. Balling my fists in the bedsheets, I cried out in pleasure, I biting my tongue to try and stop from behind too loud. The lawyer twisted his fingers into my hair and pulled me back, my back arching as he bent over me to whisper in my ear. 'I want to fucking hear you.' He growled.

I let my mouth drop open, moaning and screaming in pleasure as both men chased their own orgasms, mine fast approaching. When my orgasm finally came crashing down, I could only focus on that as it ripped through me. The overwhelming pleasure was dragged out for as long as possible with two cocks still thrusting into me, I couldn't do anything but let them use me as they pleased.

The lawyer pulling out of me was a shock, my ass twitching at the sudden loss of fullness. I heard him let out a low growl as he finally came, ribbons of cum shooting across my back and my ass. Beneath me the doctor continued to thrust, holding me down on his pelvis as he finished inside me, his fingers digging into my skin.

I collapsed onto the doctor's chest, catching my breath as the lawyer got off the bed. I relaxed as I felt the doctor rub his thumbs across my hips until the lawyer returned with a wet washcloth and rubbed it across my back. He gently rolled me off his friend, covering me with a blanket as they pulled their clothes back on.

'Amazing night.' The doctor whispered, pressing a kiss to my forehead.

Two business cards were dropped onto the bedside table.

'12 pm check out tomorrow. The shower in the bathroom is amazing.' The lawyer smiled. With both men completely dressed, they each pressed a kiss to my lips and gave me a smile.

'Call us again sometime. Together or separately.' The doctor smirked, walking out of the door, closely followed by the lawyer.

Alone, I stretched out across the mattress, I could feel what they had left me. I look at the business cards on the side, each with a personal phone number scribbled on the back.

That would be happening again.

Aftercare

'*CUCUMBER*!'

It was muffled but distinct. Everything stopped. There were no more lashes, the pain stopped. The only sound left into the room was her small cries as she tried to hold them in. There was an echo as the whip hit the floor and she flinched, the so finally passing her lips. His fingers gently touched her skir moving over her hips and stomach. Her whole body trembled She slowly calmed as she felt his fingers and listened to hi voice.

'Focus on where my fingers are, where my hands are His palm lay flat across her stomach, his other hand rubbin small circles on her arm. Her breathing slowed, taking dee breaths as he moved around her body, kneeling behind her. On had stayed on her stomach, calming her breathing until the tear stopped. His other hand rubbed across her shoulders, slowl moving closer to her until her back was pressed against his chest.

'Just breath, calmly.' He whispered; his breath was hot against her ear. She slowly nodded, taking in large, shaky breaths.

He stood and moved in front of her. Both of his hands on her arms, gently rubbing up and down. Her breathing calmed. He didn't say anything after that. He listened to her as she calmed down.

'Are you okay?' His voice was quiet, soothing. He bent down over her kneeling form and reached behind her to unbuckle the ring gag that prevented her from speaking, her jaw ached from being propped open so long. She gently swallowed, her throat hoarse from the previous play.

'Honey?' He gently pushed the blindfold off her eyes and over her head. The room was dim, a lamp in the corner illuminated her surroundings gently, allowing her eyes to adjust more easily. 'Nod if you're okay?' He whispered; the corner of her lips curved upwards as she gave a slight nod.

He gently removed the nipple clamps, but she flinched, she had gotten used to the pain they gave, but now the freedom was much worse. He moved behind her and began to untie the knots at her back. They kept her in position, each hand holding the opposite elbow. The rope wrapped around her chest and was pleasurably tight around her breasts. The rope loosened and began a pile on the floor, she tentatively flexed her muscles, stretching out her arms and rolling her shoulders.

He gathered up the ropes and discarded them back into the box, he got up and disappeared into the en-suite and returned moments later with a glass of water, bottle of lotion, and warm, wet flannel. He placed them on the bedside table and moved to her.

He leaned down and wrapped his arms around her back, she instinctively wrapped her arms around his neck, allowing him to pick her up comfortably and take her to the bed. The soft covers brushed against her sore skin.

Heavenly.

He rearranged the pillows and leaned her against the headboard, handing her the glass of water. She took it eagerly, gulping down the cool soothing liquid.

He grabbed the flannel and began to wipe it across her body, clearing all the sweat and cum from her skin, careful to avoid the angry red marks that the ropes had created. Once he was satisfied, he dropped the flannel onto the side table and picked up the bottle of lotion; gently massaging it in; a soft sigh left her lips as she felt it soothe her burning muscles. He watched as her eyelids began to fall, she tried so desperately to stay awake.

He put the lotion with the flannel and moved up the bed, she immediately began to curl into him. He wrapped his arms around her, drawing light patterns on her bare back.

'You did so well today.' He whispered, feeling her beginning to drop off to sleep on his chest. 'Such a good girl.'

'Hmmm.' She replied sleepily.

'You're safe here. You did so well today.' He praised her again and again until she drifted off to sleep to the sound of his voice.

Printed in Great Britain
by Amazon